Sweet As Can Bee

KATHERINE CAMPOS LOZANO

Scripture quotations marked (NLT) are taken from the Holy Bible, New Living Translation, copyright © 1996, 2004, 2007 by Tyndale House Foundation. Used by permission of Tyndale House Publishers, Inc., Carol Stream, Illinois 60188. All rights reserved.

Scripture taken from the Holy Bible, NEW INTERNATIONAL VERSION®. Copyright © 1973, 1978, 1984 by Biblica, Inc. All rights reserved worldwide. Used by permission. NEW INTERNATIONAL VERSION® and NIV® are registered trademarks of Biblica, Inc. Use of either trademark for the offering of goods or services requires the prior written consent of Biblica US, Inc.

WestBow Press books may be ordered through booksellers or by contacting:

WestBow Press
A Division of Thomas Nelson & Zondervan
1663 Liberty Drive
Bloomington, IN 47403
www.westbowpress.com
1 (866) 928-1240

Because of the dynamic nature of the Internet, any web addresses or links contained in this book may have changed since publication and may no longer be valid. The views expressed in this work are solely those of the author and do not necessarily reflect the views of the publisher, and the publisher hereby disclaims any responsibility for them.

Any people depicted in stock imagery provided by Getty Images are models, and such images are being used for illustrative purposes only.
Certain stock imagery © Getty Images.

ISBN: 978-1-9736-4970-0 (sc)
ISBN: 978-1-9736-4971-7 (e)

Library of Congress Control Number: 2018915026

Print information available on the last page.

WestBow Press rev. date: 2/20/2019

Sweet as Can Bee

~ written and illustrated
by Katherine Campos Lozano

for M.F.H. with love.

Once upon a time, somewhere between the hills and valleys, there was a little cave. And in that little cave...

...lived Caramel and Honey Bear.

And they loved each other...

Very much.

They ate honeycomb together.

They swam together in the Lakes of Blue.

And they took naps together all the time.

One morning Honey woke up to the sound of
a little bee buzzing by his ear.

"Why, good morning Canary," Honey said to the bee. "What a beautiful morning," he thought to himself. He looked over to Caramel, who was still sleeping. Honey smiled and thought, "Well I'm going to gather some breakfast for us now."

Before getting up, Honey thanked and prayed to the Lord. He smiled and said, "Dear Lord, thank you for this brand new day. Please make today special for Caramel and me. Amen."

So Honey took a few steps outside the cave and took a breath of fresh air. Canary flew and buzzed near Honey's ear again, "Maybe you can lead me to the honeycomb." Honey said to the little bee. And so Canary lead the way.

The little bee started to fly really high towards a rose blossom tree. Honey gazed up in confusion. "There doesn't seem to be any honeycomb up in this tree," He said. But the little bee was about to show him something sweeter.

And at the top of that tree, there was a beautiful rose bloomed in the shape of a heart. Honey's eyes widened with awe.

As he gazed, he thought of Caramel and how much he wanted
to get it for her. The problem was that it was really really
high up. He had to think of a way to get it before Caramel
woke up. But Honey has never climbed that high.

The tree was also very wide. He couldn't get a firm grip
on the tree to climb it. So he ran to the store really quick
to buy some balloons. . . He blew them up and tied them to
his waist. And he started to fly up and up and up...

Honey tried many times. He flew up but a tree branch popped the balloons and he gently floated back down. He tried a ladder, but it was too short. He tried to throw a rope around the rose blossom to pull it down, but the rope got tangled around a branch and pulled down a pile of leaves instead.

Meanwhile... back at the cave, Caramel
awoke and called out, "Honey?"

Honey saw no way of reaching that rose blossom upon the tree. And he felt sad. So he sighed, "Lord, this was supposed to be a special day for me and Caramel... please help me."

The Lord heard Honey's prayer and smiled down from Heaven. So the Lord sent a strong gust of wind. And He commanded the wind to shake the rose blossom tree...

"Trust in the Lord with all your heart and lean not
on your own understanding." -Proverbs 3:5

And the rose blossom came loose and
flew down with the breeze.

Honey ran after the rose blossom and it landed safely on the pile of leaves that Honey's rope pulled down earlier.

Honey was overjoyed and laughed, "Ahaha! Thank you Lord!"
and he pounced on the flower, landing in the big pile of leaves.

Caramel went out to look for Honey. "Honey, where are you?" She said in a curious voice. She kept looking.

"Hm?"

"What are you doing in there sweetheart?" Caramel
asked as Honey peeked from the leaves.

Honey then jumped out and surprised Caramel with his gift.

Caramel was so happy and she turned bright pink.
She jumped from so much joy to hug Honey.

They were both very grateful and they enjoyed the rest of the afternoon together. Honey put the flower in Caramel's fur behind her ear. They both ate honeycomb and grew more and more in love. And life was as sweet as can bee!

Printed in the United States
By Bookmasters